John Keats

Roses of Romance from the Poems of John Keats

John Keats

Roses of Romance from the Poems of John Keats

ISBN/EAN: 9783337049393

Printed in Europe, USA, Canada, Australia, Japan

Cover: Foto ©Andreas Hilbeck / pixelio.de

More available books at **www.hansebooks.com**

ISABELLA.

ROSES·OF·ROMANCE

FROM·THE·POEMS·OF
JOHN·KEATS

SELECTED·AND·ILLUSTRATED·BY
EDMUND·H·GARRETT

ROBERTS·BROTHERS

BOSTON

M·D·CCC·LXXXXI

KEATS

1796   1820

"Till the future dares
Forget the past, his fate and fame shall be
An echo and a light unto eternity"

From Adonais an elegy
on the death of JOHN KEATS
by Percy Bysshe Shelley

Contents

LIST OF ILLUSTRATIONS

La belle dame sans merci

La Belle Dame — Sans Merc

I.

AH, what can ail thee, wretched wight,
  Alone and palely loitering?
The sedge is wither'd from the lake,
  And no birds sing.

13

La Belle Dame sans Merci.

II.

Ah, what can ail thee, wretched wight,
  So haggard and so woe-begone?
The squirrel's granary is full,
  And the harvest's done.

III.

I see a lily on thy brow,
  With anguish moist and fever dew;
And on thy cheek a fading rose
  Fast withereth too.

IV.

I met a lady in the meads
  Full beautiful, a faery's child;
Her hair was long, her foot was light,
  And her eyes were wild.

V.

I set her on my pacing steed,
  And nothing else saw all day long;
For sideways would she lean, and sing
  A faery's song.

"HER HAIR WAS LONG, HER FOOT WAS LIGHT."

La Belle Dame sans Merci.

VI.

I made a garland for her head,
    And bracelets too, and fragrant zone;
She look'd at me as she did love,
    And made sweet moan.

VII.

She found me roots of relish sweet,
    And honey wild, and manna dew;
And sure in language strange she said,
    "I love thee true!"

VIII.

She took me to her elfin grot,
    And there she gaz'd and sighed deep,
And there I shut her wild sad eyes
    So kiss'd to sleep.

IX.

And there we slumber'd on the moss,
    And there I dream'd, ah, woe betide,
The latest dream I ever dream'd
    On the cold hill side.

"I SET HER ON MY PACING STEED."

La Belle Dame sans Merci.

X.

I saw pale kings, and princes too,
 Pale warriors, death-pale were they all;
Who cry'd—"La Belle Dame sans merci
 Hath thee in thrall!"

XI.

I saw their starv'd lips in the gloom
 With horrid warning gaped wide,
And I awoke, and found me here
 On the cold hill side.

XII.

And this is why I sojourn here
 Alone and palely loitering,
Though the sedge is wither'd from the lake,
 And no birds sing.

ISABELLA
A·STORY·FROM
BOCCACCIO

Isabella

OR, THE POT OF BASIL.

A STORY, FROM BOCCACCIO.

I.

FAIR Isabel, poor simple Isabel!
　　Lorenzo, a young palmer in Love's eye!
They could not in the self-same mansion dwell
　　Without some stir of heart, some malady;

Isabella; or, the Pot of Basil.

They could not sit at meals but feel how well
   It soothed each to be the other by;
They could not, sure, beneath the same roof sleep
But to each other dream, and nightly weep.

II.

With every morn their love grew tenderer,
   With every eve deeper and tenderer still;
He might not in house, field, or garden stir,
   But her full shape would all his seeing fill;
And his continual voice was pleasanter
   To her than noise of trees or hidden rill;
Her lute-string gave an echo of his name,
She spoilt her half-done broidery with the same.

III.

He knew whose gentle hand was at the latch,
   Before the door had given her to his eyes;
And from her chamber-window he would catch
   Her beauty farther than the falcon spies;
And constant as her vespers would he watch,
   Because her face was turn'd to the same skies;
And with sick longing all the night outwear,
To hear her morning-step upon the stair.

IV.

A whole long month of May in this sad plight
  Made their cheeks paler by the break of June:
"To-morrow will I bow to my delight,
  To-morrow will I ask my lady's boon." —
"O may I never see another night,
  Lorenzo, if thy lips breathe not love's tune." —
So spake they to their pillows; but, alas,
Honeyless days and days did he let pass;

V.

Until sweet Isabella's untouch'd cheek
  Fell sick within the rose's just domain,
Fell thin as a young mother's, who doth seek
  By every lull to cool her infant's pain:
"How ill she is," said he, "I may not speak,
  And yet I will, and tell my love all plain:
If looks speak love-laws, I will drink her tears,
And at the least 't will startle off her cares."

VI.

So said he one fair morning, and all day
  His heart beat awfully against his side;
And to his heart he inwardly did pray
  For power to speak; but still the ruddy tide

Isabella; or, the Pot of Basil.

Stifled his voice, and puls'd resolve away —
  Fever'd his high conceit of such a bride,
Yet brought him to the meekness of a child:
Alas! when passion is both meek and wild!

VII.

So once more he had wak'd and anguished
  A dreary night of love and misery,
If Isabel's quick eye had not been wed
  To every symbol on his forehead high;
She saw it waxing very pale and dead,
  And straight all flush'd; so, lisped tenderly,
"Lorenzo!" — here she ceas'd her timid quest,
But in her tone and look he read the rest.

VIII.

" O Isabella, I can half perceive
  That I may speak my grief into thine ear;
If thou didst ever anything believe,
  Believe how I love thee, believe how near
My soul is to its doom: I would not grieve
  Thy hand by unwelcome pressing, would not fear
Thine eyes by gazing; but I cannot live
Another night, and not my passion shrive.

IX.

"Love, thou art leading me from wintry cold!
 Lady, thou leadest me to summer clime!
And I must taste the blossoms that unfold
 In its ripe warmth this gracious morning time."
So said, his erewhile timid lips grew bold,
 And poesied with hers in dewy rhyme.
Great bliss was with them, and great happiness
Grew like a lusty flower in June's caress.

X.

Parting they seem'd to tread upon the air,
 Twin roses by the zephyr blown apart
Only to meet again more close, and share
 The inward fragrance of each other's heart.
She, to her chamber gone, a ditty fair
 Sang, of delicious love and honey'd dart;
He with light steps went up a western hill,
And bade the sun farewell, and joy'd his fill.

XI.

All close they met again, before the dusk
 Had taken from the stars its pleasant veil,
All close they met, all eves, before the dusk
 Had taken from the stars its pleasant veil,

Close in a bower of hyacinth and musk,
  Unknown of any, free from whispering tale.
Ah, better had it been forever so,
Than idle ears should pleasure in their woe!

XII.

Were they unhappy then? It cannot be—
  Too many tears for lovers have been shed,
Too many sighs give we to them in fee,
  Too much of pity after they are dead,
Too many doleful stories do we see,
  Whose matter in bright gold were best be read;
Except in such a page where Theseus' spouse
Over the pathless waves towards him bows.

XIII.

But, for the general award of love,
  The little sweet doth kill much bitterness;
Though Dido silent is in under-grove,
  And Isabella's was a great distress,
Though young Lorenzo in warm Indian clove
  Was not embalm'd, this truth is not the less—
Even bees, the little almsmen of spring-bowers
Know there is richest juice in poison-flowers.

XIV.

With her two brothers this fair lady dwelt,
  Enriched from ancestral merchandise,
And for them many a weary hand did swelt
  In torched mines and noisy factories,
And many once proud-quiver'd loins did melt
  In blood from stinging whip; with hollow eyes
Many all day in dazzling river stood,
To take the rich-or'd driftings of the flood.

XV.

For them the Ceylon diver held his breath,
  And went all naked to the hungry shark;
For them his ears gush'd blood; for them in death
  The seal on the cold ice with piteous bark
Lay full of darts; for them alone did seethe
  A thousand men in troubles wide and dark:
Half-ignorant, they turn'd an easy wheel,
That set sharp racks at work, to pinch and peel.

XVI.

Why were they proud? Because their marble
    founts
  Gush'd with more pride than do a wretch's
    tears? —

27

Isabella; or, the Pot of Basil.

Why were they proud? Because fair orange
   mounts
  Were of more soft ascent than lazar stairs?—
Why were they proud? Because red-lin'd accounts
  Were richer than the songs of Grecian years?—
Why were they proud; again we ask aloud,
Why in the name of Glory were they proud?

XVII.

Yet were these Florentines as self-retir'd
  In hungry pride and gainful cowardice,
As two close Hebrews in that land inspir'd,
  Pal'd in and vineyarded from beggar-spies;
The hawks of ship-mast forests — the untir'd
  And pannier'd mules for ducats and old lies —
Quick cat's-paws on the generous stray-away,—
Great wits in Spanish, Tuscan, and Malay.

XVIII.

How was it these same ledger-men could spy
  Fair Isabella in her downy nest?
How could they find out in Lorenzo's eye
  A straying from his toil? Hot Egypt's pest
Into their vision covetous and sly!
  How could these money-bags see east and west?

Yet so they did — and every dealer fair
Must see behind, as doth the hunted hare.

XIX.

O eloquent and fam'd Boccaccio!
  Of thee we now should ask forgiving boon,
And of thy spicy myrtles as they blow,
  And of thy roses amorous of the moon,
And of thy lilies, that do paler grow
  Now they can no more hear thy ghittern's
    tune,
For venturing syllables that ill beseem
The quiet glooms of such a piteous theme.

XX.

Grant thou a pardon here, and then the tale
  Shall move on soberly, as it is meet;
There is no other crime, no mad assail
  To make old prose in modern rhyme more
    sweet:
But it is done — succeed the verse or fail —
  To honor thee, and thy gone spirit greet;
To stead thee as a verse in English tongue,
An echo of thee in the north-wind sung.

Isabella ; or, the Pot of Basil.

XXI.

These brethren having found by many signs
  What love Lorenzo for their sister had,
And how she lov'd him too, each unconfines
  His bitter thoughts to other, well nigh mad
That he, the servant of their trade designs,
  Should in their sister's love be blithe and glad,
When 't was their plan to coax her by degrees
To some high noble and his olive-trees.

XXII.

And many a jealous conference had they,
  And many times they bit their lips alone,
Before they fix'd upon a surest way
  To make the youngster for his crime atone;
And at the last, these men of cruel clay
  Cut Mercy with a sharp knife to the bone;
For they resolved in some forest dim
To kill Lorenzo, and there bury him.

XXIII.

So on a pleasant morning, as he leant
  Into the sun-rise, o'er the balustrade
Of the garden-terrace, towards him they bent
  Their footing through the dews; and to him
    said,   30

" You seem there in the quiet of content,
  Lorenzo, and we are most loth to invade
Calm speculation; but if you are wise,
Bestride your steed while cold is in the skies.

XXIV.

" To-day we purpose, aye, this hour we mount
  To spur three leagues towards the Apennine;
Come down, we pray thee, ere the hot sun count
  His dewy rosary on the eglantine."
Lorenzo, courteously as he was wont,
  Bow'd a fair greeting to these serpents' whine;
And went in haste, to get in readiness,
With belt and spur and bracing huntsman's dress.

XXV.

And as he to the court-yard pass'd along,
  Each third step did he pause, and listen'd oft
If he could hear his lady's matin-song,
  Or the light whisper of her footstep soft;
And as he thus over his passion hung,
  He heard a laugh full musical aloft;
When, looking up, he saw her features bright
Smile through an in-door lattice, all delight.

Isabella; or, the Pot of Basil.

XXVI.

" Love, Isabel!" said he, "I was in pain
  Lest I should miss to bid thee a good morrow:
Ah, what if I should lose thee, when so fain
  I am to stifle all the heavy sorrow
Of a poor three hours' absence? But we'll gain
  Out of the amorous dark what day doth
    borrow.
Good-by! I'll soon be back." — "Good-by!"
    said she: —
And as he went she chanted merrily.

XXVII.

So the two brothers and their murder'd man
  Rode past fair Florence, to where Arno's
    stream
Gurgles through straiten'd banks, and still doth
    fan
  Itself with dancing bulrush, and the bream
Keeps head against the freshets. Sick and wan
  The brothers' faces in the ford did seem,
Lorenzo's flush with love. They pass'd the
    water
Into a forest quiet for the slaughter.

32

Isabella; or, the Pot of Basil.

XXVIII.

There was Lorenzo slain and buried in,
  There in that forest did his great love cease;
Ah, when a soul doth thus its freedom win,
  It aches in loneliness — is ill at peace
As the break-covert blood-hounds of such sin!
  They dipp'd their swords in the water, and did
    tease
Their horses homeward, with convulsed spur,
Each richer by his being a murderer.

XXIX.

They told their sister how, with sudden speed,
  Lorenzo had ta'en ship for foreign lands,
Because of some great urgency and need
  In their affairs, requiring trusty hands.
Poor girl, put on thy stifling widow's weed,
  And 'scape at once from Hope's accursed bands;
To-day thou wilt not see him, nor to-morrow,
And the next day will be a day of sorrow!

XXX.

She weeps alone for pleasures not to be;
  Sorely she wept until the night came on,

Isabella; or, the Pot of Basil.

And then, instead of love, O misery!
  She brooded o'er the luxury alone
His image in the dusk she seem'd to see,
  And to the silence made a gentle moan,
Spreading her perfect arms upon the air,
And on her couch low murmuring, "Where? O
    where?"

XXXI.

But Selfishness, Love's cousin, held not long
  Its fiery vigil in her single breast;
She fretted for the golden hour, and hung
  Upon the time with feverish unrest,
Not long, for soon into her heart a throng
  Of higher occupants, a richer zest,
Came tragic; passion not to be subdu'd,
And sorrow for her love in travels rude.

XXXII.

In the mid days of autumn, on their eves
  The breath of Winter comes from far away,
And the sick west continually bereaves
  Of some gold tinge, and plays a roundelay
Of death among the bushes and the leaves,
  To make all bare before he dares to stray

From his north cavern. So sweet Isabel
By gradual decay from beauty fell,

XXXIII.

Because Lorenzo came not. Oftentimes
    She ask'd her brothers, with an eye all pale,
Striving to be itself, what dungeon climes
    Could keep him off so long? They spake a
            tale
Time after time, to quiet her. Their crimes
    Came on them, like a smoke from Hinnom's
            vale;
And every night in dreams they groan'd aloud,
To see their sister in her snowy shroud,

XXXIV.

And she had died in drowsy ignorance,
    But for a thing more deadly dark than all;
It came like a fierce potion, drunk by chance,
    Which saves a sick man from the feather'd pall
For some few gasping moments; like a lance,
    Waking an Indian from his cloudy hall
With cruel pierce, and bringing him again
Sense of the gnawing fire at heart and brain.

35

XXXV.

It was a vision. In the drowsy gloom,
   The dull of midnight, at her couch's foot
Lorenzo stood, and wept: the forest tomb
   Had marr'd his glossy hair which once could
       shoot
Lustre into the sun, and put cold doom
   Upon his lips, and taken the soft lute
From his lorn voice, and past his loamed ears
Had made a miry channel for his tears.

XXXVI.

Strange sound it was, when the pale shadow spake ;
   For there was striving, in its piteous tongue,
To speak as when on earth it was awake,
   And Isabella on its music hung :
Languor there was in it, and tremulous shake,
   As in a palsied Druid's harp unstrung ;
And though it moaned a ghostly under-song,
Like hoarse night-gusts sepulchral briers among.

XXXVII.

Its eyes, though wild, were still all dewy bright
   With love, and kept all·phantom fear aloof

Isabella; or, the Pot of Basil.

From the poor girl by magic of their light,
    The while it did unthread the horrid woof
Of the late darkn'd time,—the murderous spite
    Of pride and avarice, the dark pine roof
In the forest, and the sodden turfed dell,
Where, without any word, from stabs he fell.

XXXVIII.

Saying moreover, "Isabel, my sweet,
    Red whortle-berries droop above my head,
And a large flint-stone weighs upon my feet;
    Around me beeches and high chestnuts shed
Their leaves and prickly nuts; a sheep-fold bleat
    Comes from beyond the river to my bed.
Go, shed one tear upon my heather-bloom,
And it shall comfort me within the tomb.

XXXIX.

"I am a shadow now, alas! alas!
    Upon the skirts of human nature dwelling
Alone: I chant alone the holy Mass,
    While little sounds of life are round me knelling,
And glossy bees at noon do fieldward pass,
    And many a chapel bell the hour is telling,

37

Paining me through: those sounds grow strange
    to me,
And thou art distant in Humanity.

XL.

"I know what was, I feel full well what is,
    And I should rage, if spirits could go mad,
Though I forget the taste of earthly bliss,
    That paleness warms my grave, as though I had
A Seraph chosen from the bright abyss
    To be my spouse: thy paleness makes me glad;
Thy beauty grows upon me and I feel
A greater love through all my essence steal."

XLI.

The Spirit mourn'd, "Adieu!" — dissolv'd, and
    left
    The atom darkness in a slow turmoil;
As when of healthful midnight sleep bereft,
    Thinking on rugged hours and fruitless toil,
We put our eyes into a pillowy cleft,
    And see the spangly gloom froth up and boil.
It made sad Isabella's eyelids ache,
And in the dawn she started up awake.

"RESOLVED, SHE TOOK WITH HER AN AGED NURSE."

XLII.

"Ha! ha!" said she, "I knew not this hard life;
  I thought the worst was simple misery;
I thought some Fate with pleasure or with strife
  Portion'd us—happy days, or else to die;
But there is crime—a brother's bloody knife!
  Sweet Spirit, thou hast school'd my infancy:
I'll visit thee for this, and kiss thine eyes,
And greet thee morn and even in the skies."

XLIII.

When the full morning came, she had devised
  How she might secret to the forest hie;
How she might find the clay, so dearly prized,
  And sing to it one latest lullaby;
How her short absence might be unsurmised,
  While she the inmost of the dream would try.
Resolved, she took with her an aged nurse,
And went into that dismal forest-hearse.

XLIV.

See, as they creep along the river side,
  How she doth whisper to that aged Dame,
And, after looking round the champaign wide,
  Shows her a knife.—"What feverous hectic flame

Burns in thee, child ? — what good can thee betide,
   That thou should'st smile again ? "   The evening
      came,
And they had found Lorenzo's earthy bed;
The flint was there, the berries at his head.

XLV.

Who hath not loiter'd in a green church-yard,
   And let his spirit, like a demon mole,
Work through the clayey soil and gravel hard,
   To see skull, coffin'd bones, and funeral stole;
Pitying each form that hungry Death hath marr'd,
   And filling it once more with human soul?
Ah, this is holiday to what was felt
When Isabella by Lorenzo knelt !

XLVI.

She gazed into the fresh-thrown mould, as though
   One glance did fully all its secrets tell;
Clearly she saw, as other eyes would know
   Pale limbs at bottom of a crystal well;
Upon the murderous spot she seem'd to grow,
   Like to a native lily of the dell :
Then with her knife, all sudden she began
To dig more fervently than misers can.

H

Isabella; or, the Pot of Basil.

XLVII.

Soon she turn'd up a soiled glove, whereon
  Her silk had play'd in purple fantasies;
She kiss'd it with a lip more chill than stone,
  And put it in her bosom, where it dries
And freezes utterly unto the bone
  Those dainties made to still an infant's cries:
Then 'gan she work again; nor stay'd her care,
But to throw back at times her veiling hair.

XLVIII.

That old nurse stood beside her wondering,
  Until her heart felt pity to the core
At sight of such a dismal laboring,
  And so she kneeled, with her locks all hoar,
And put her lean hands to the horrid thing.
  Three hours they labor'd at this travail sore;
At last they felt the kernel of the grave,
And Isabella did not stamp and rave.

XLIX.

Ah, wherefore all this wormy circumstance?
  Why linger at the yawning tomb so long?
O for the gentleness of old Romance,
  The simple plaining of a minstrel's song!

Isabella; or, the Pot of Basil.

Fair reader, at the old tale take a glance,
 For here, in truth, it doth not well belong
To speak:—O turn thee to the very tale,
And taste the music of that vision pale.

L.

With duller steel than the Perséan sword
 They cut away no formless monster's head,
But one, whose gentleness did well accord
 With death, as life. The ancient harps have said,
Love never dies, but lives, immortal Lord.
 If Love impersonate was ever dead,
Pale Isabella kiss'd it, and low moan'd.
'T was love; cold,—dead indeed, but not de-
 thron'd.

LI.

In anxious secrecy they took it home,
 And then the prize was all for Isabel.
She calm'd its wild hair with a golden comb,
 And all around each eye's sepulchral cell
Pointed each fringed lash; the smeared loam
 With tears, as chilly as a dripping well,
She drench'd away:—and still she comb'd and kept
Sighing all day; and still she kiss'd, and wept.

Esabella ; or, the Pot of Basil.

LII.

Then in a silken scarf, — sweet with the dews
   Of precious flowers pluck'd in Araby,
And divine liquids come with odorous ooze
   Through the cold serpent-pipe refreshfully, —
She wrapp'd it up; and for its tomb did choose
   A garden-pot, wherein she laid it by,
And cover'd it with mould, and o'er it set
Sweet Basil, which her tears kept ever wet.

LIII.

And she forgot the stars, the moon, and sun,
   And she forgot the blue above the trees,
And she forgot the dells where waters run,
   And she forgot the chilly autumn breeze;
She had no knowledge when the day was done,
   And the new morn she saw not: but in peace
Hung over her sweet Basil evermore,
And moisten'd it with tears unto the core.

LIV.

And so she ever fed it with thin tears,
   Whence thick and green and beautiful it grew,
So that it smelt more balmy than its peers
   Of Basil-tufts in Florence; for it drew

Isabella; or, the Pot of Basil.

Nurture besides, and life, from human fears,
  From the fast mouldering head there shut from
    view:
So that the jewel, safely casketed,
Came forth, and in perfumed leaflets spread.

LV.

O Melancholy, linger here awhile!
  O Music, Music, breathe despondingly!
O Echo, Echo, from some sombre isle,
  Unknown, Lethean, sigh to us — O sigh!
Spirits in grief, lift up your heads, and smile;
  Lift up your heads, sweet Spirits, heavily,
And make a pale light in your cypress
    glooms,
Tinting with silver wan your marble tombs.

LVI.

Moan hither, all ye syllables of woe,
  From the deep throat of sad Melpomene!
Through bronzed lyre in tragic order go,
  And touch the strings into a mystery;
Sound mournfully upon the winds and low;
  For simple Isabel is soon to be

Among the dead: She withers, like a palm,
Cut by an Indian for its juicy balm.

LVII.

O leave the palm to wither by itself;
  Let not quick Winter chill its dying hour!
It may not be — those Baälites of pelf,
  Her brethren, noted the continual shower
From her dead eyes; and many a curious elf,
  Among her kindred, wonder'd that such dower
Of youth and beauty should be thrown aside
By one mark'd out to be a Noble's bride.

LVIII.

And, furthermore, her brethren wonder'd much
  Why she sat drooping by the Basil green,
And why it flourish'd, as by magic touch;
  Greatly they wonder'd what the thing might
    mean.
They could not surely give belief that such
  A very nothing would have power to wean
Her from her own fair youth, and pleasures
    gay,
And even remembrance of her love's delay.

LIX.

Therefore they watch'd a time when they might sift
    This hidden whim; and long they watch'd in vain;
For seldom did she go to chapel-shrift,
    And seldom felt she any hunger-pain;
And when she left, she hurried back, as swift
    As bird on wing to breast its eggs again;
And, patient as a hen-bird, sat her there
Besides her Basil, weeping through her hair.

LX.

Yet they contriv'd to steal the Basil-pot,
    And to examine it in secret place.
The thing was vile with green and livid spot,
    And yet they knew it was Lorenzo's face:
The guerdon of their murder they had got,
    And so left Florence in a moment's space,
Never to turn again. Away they went,
With blood upon their heads, to banishment.

LXI.

O Melancholy, turn thine eyes away!
    O Music, Music, breathe despondingly!
O Echo, Echo, on some other day,
    From isles Lethean, sigh to us — O sigh!

47

Isabella; or, the Pot of Basil.

Spirits of grief, sing not your " Well-a-way ! "
  For Isabel, sweet Isabel, will die;
Will die a death too lone and incomplete,
Now they have ta'en away her Basil sweet.

LXII.

Piteous she look'd on dead and senseless things,
  Asking for her lost Basil amorously;
And with melodious chuckle in the strings
  Of her lorn voice, she oftentimes would cry
After the Pilgrim in his wanderings,
  To ask him where her Basil was; and why
'T was hid from her: " For cruel 't is," said she,
" To steal my Basil-pot away from me."

LXIII.

And so she pin'd, and so she died forlorn,
  Imploring for her Basil to the last.
No heart was there in Florence but did mourn
  In pity of her love, so overcast.
And a sad ditty of this story born
  From mouth to mouth through all the country
    pass'd :
Still is the burthen sung — " O cruelty,
To steal my Basil-pot away from me ! "

THE·EVE·OF·SAINT·AGNES

✝

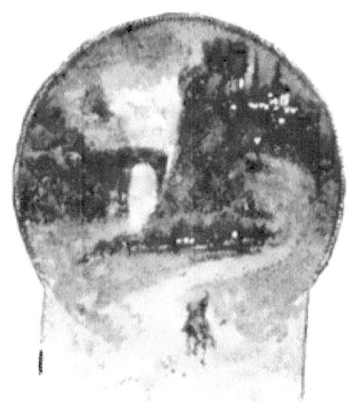

THE EVE OF SAINT AGNES

I.

SAINT AGNES' EVE — ah, bitter chill it was!
    The owl, for all his feathers, was a-cold;
The hare limp'd trembling through the frozen
    grass;
And silent was the flock in woolly fold.
Numb was the Beadsman's fingers while he told
His rosary, and while his frosted breath,
Like pious incense from a censer old,
Seem'd taking flight for heaven, without a death,
Past the sweet Virgin's picture, while his prayer
    he saith.

II.

His prayer he saith, this patient, holy man,
Then takes his lamp, and riseth from his knees,
And back returneth, meagre, barefoot, wan,
Along the chapel aisle by slow degrees.
The sculptur'd dead, on each side, seem to freeze,
Emprison'd in black, purgatorial rails:
Knights, ladies, praying in dumb orat'ries,
He passeth by; and his weak spirit fails
To think how they may ache in icy hoods and
    mails.

III.

Northward he turneth through a little door,
And scarce three steps, ere Music's golden
    tongue
Flatter'd to tears this aged man and poor;
But no — already had his death-bell rung;
The joys of all his life were said and sung:
His was harsh penance on Saint Agnes' Eve.
Another way he went, and soon among
Rough ashes sat he for his soul's reprieve,
And all night kept awake, for sinners' sake to
    grieve.

IV.

That ancient Beadsman heard the prelude soft;
And so it chanc'd, for many a door was wide
From hurry to and fro. Soon, up aloft,
The silver, snarling trumpets 'gan to chide;
The level chambers, ready with their pride,
Were glowing to receive a thousand guests;
The carved angels, ever eager-ey'd,
Star'd, where upon their heads the cornice rests,
With hair blown black, and wings put cross-wise
    on their breasts.

V.

At length burst in the argent revelry,
With plume, tiara, and all rich array,
Numerous as shadows haunting faerily
The brain, new-stuff'd, in youth, with triumphs
    gay
Of old romance. These let us wish away,
And turn, sole-thoughted, to one Lady there,
Whose heart had brooded, all that wintry day,
On love, and wing'd Saint Agnes' saintly care,
As she had heard old dames full many times
    declare.

The Eve of Saint Agnes.

They told her how, upon Saint Agnes' Eve,
Young virgins might have visions of delight,
And soft adorings from their loves receive
Upon the honey'd middle of the night,
If ceremonies due they did aright;
As, supperless to bed they must retire,
And couch supine their beauties, lily white;
Nor look behind, nor sideways, but require
Of Heaven with upward eyes for all that they
    desire.

VII

Full of this whim was thoughtful Madeline.
The music yearning like a God in pain,
She scarcely heard; her maiden eyes divine,
Fix'd on the floor, saw many a sweeping train
Pass by — she heeded not at all. In vain
Came many a tiptoe, amorous cavalier,
And back retir'd, not cool'd by high disdain;
But she saw not: her heart was otherwhere;
She sigh'd for Agnes' dreams, the sweetest of the
    year.

"CAME MANY A TIPTOE, AMOROUS CAVALIER."

VIII.

She danced along with vague, regardless eyes,
Anxious her lips, her breathing quick and
    short;
The hallow'd hour was near at hand. She sighs
Amid the timbrels, and the throng'd resort
Of whisperers in anger, or in sport;
'Mid looks of love, defiance, hate, and scorn,
Hoodwink'd with faery fancy; all amort,
Save to Saint Agnes and her lambs unshorn,
And all the bliss to be before to-morrow morn.

IX.

So, purposing each moment to retire,
She linger'd still.   Meantime, across the moors,
Had come young Porphyro, with heart on fire
For Madeline. Beside the portal doors,
Buttress'd from moonlight, stands he, and
    implores
All saints to give him sight of Madeline,
But for one moment in the tedious hours,
That he might gaze and worship all unseen;
Perchance speak, kneel, touch, kiss — in sooth such
    things have been.

X.

He ventures in: let no buzz'd whisper tell,
All eyes be muffled, or a hundred swords
Will storm his heart, Love's fev'rous citadel.
For him, those chambers held barbarian hordes,
Hyena foemen, and hot-blooded lords,
Whose very dogs would execrations howl
Against his lineage: not one breast affords
Him any mercy, in that mansion foul,
Save one old beldame, weak in body and in soul.

XI.

Ah, happy chance! The aged creature came,
Shuffling along with ivory-headed wand,
To where he stood, hid from the torch's
        flame,
Behind a broad hall-pillar, far beyond
The sound of merriment and chorus bland.
He startled her; but soon she knew his face,
And grasp'd his fingers in her palsied hand,
Saying, " Mercy, Porphyro, hie thee from this
        place;
They are all here to-night, the whole blood-thirsty
        race !

XII.

"Get hence! get hence! there's dwarfish Hilde-
    brand;
He had a fever late, and in the fit
He cursed thee and thine, both house and land.
Then there's that old Lord Maurice, not a whit
More tame for his gray hairs — Alas me, flit!
Flit like a ghost away." "Ah, Gossip dear,
We're safe enough; here in this arm-chair sit,
And tell me how —" "Good saints! not here,
    not here;
Follow me, child, or else these stones will be thy
    bier."

XIII.

He follow'd through a lowly arched way,
Brushing the cobwebs with his lofty plume;
And as she mutter'd, "Well-a-well-a-day!"
He found him in a little moonlight room,
Pale, lattic'd, chill, and silent as a tomb.
"Now tell me where is Madeline," said he,
"O tell me, Angela, by the holy loom
Which none but secret sisterhood may see,
When they Saint Agnes' wool are weaving piously."

XIV.

"Saint Agnes! Ah, it is Saint Agnes' Eve —
Yet men will murder upon holy days:
Thou must hold water in a witch's sieve,
And be liege-lord of all the Elves and Fays,
To venture so: it fills me with amaze
To see thee, Porphyro! Saint Agnes' Eve!
God's help! my lady fair the conjuror plays
This very night: good angels her deceive!
But let me laugh awhile, — I 've mickle time to
    grieve."

XV.

Feebly she laugheth in the languid moon,
While Porphyro upon her face doth look,
Like puzzled urchin on an aged crone
Who keepeth clos'd a wond'rous riddle-book,
As spectacled she sits in chimney nook.
But soon his eyes grew brilliant, when she
    told
His lady's purpose; and he scarce could brook
Tears, at the thought of those enchantments
    cold,
And Madeline asleep in lap of legends old.

The Eve of Saint Agnes.

XVI.

Sudden a thought came like a full-blown rose,
Flushing his brow, and in his pained heart
Made purple riot; then doth he propose
A stratagem, that makes the beldame start.
"A cruel man and impious thou art!
Sweet lady, let her pray and sleep and dream
Alone with her good angels, far apart
From wicked men like thee! Go, go!—I deem
Thou canst not surely be the same that thou
    didst seem."

XVII.

" I will not harm her, by all saints I swear!"
Quoth Porphyro: "O may I ne'er find grace
When my weak voice shall whisper its last
    prayer,
If one of her soft ringlets I displace,
Or look with ruffian passion in her face.
Good Angela, believe me by these tears;
Or I will, even in a moment's space,
Awake, with horrid shout, my foemen's ears,
And beard them, though they be more fang'd
    than wolves and bears."

60

XVIII.

"Ah, why wilt thou affright a feeble soul?
A poor, weak, palsy-stricken, churchyard thing,
Whose passing-bell may ere the midnight toll;
Whose prayers for thee, each morn and
    evening,
Were never miss'd." Thus plaining, doth she
    bring
A gentler speech from burning Porphyro;
So woful, and of such deep sorrowing,
That Angela gives promise she will do
Whatever he shall wish, betide her weal or woe.

XIX.

Which was, to lead him, in close secrecy,
Even to Madeline's chamber, and there hide
Him in a closet, of such privacy
That he might see her beauty unespy'd,
And win perhaps that night a peerless bride,
While legion'd faeries pac'd the coverlet,
And pale enchantment held her sleepy-ey'd.
Never on such a night have lovers met,
Since Merlin paid his Demon all the monstrous
    debt.

The Eve of Saint Agnes.

XX.

"It shall be as thou wishest," said the Dame.
"All cates and dainties shall be stored there
Quickly on this feast-night; by the tambour
    frame
Her own lute thou wilt see. No time to spare,
For I am slow and feeble, and scarce dare
On such a catering trust my dizzy head.
Wait here, my child, with patience; kneel in
    prayer
The while. Ah, thou must needs the lady wed,
Or may I never leave my grave among the dead!"

XXI.

So saying, she hobbled off with busy fear.
The lover's endless minutes slowly pass'd;
The dame return'd, and whisper'd in his ear
To follow her, with aged eyes aghast
From fright of dim espial. Safe at last,
Through many a dusky gallery, they gain
The maiden's chamber, silken, hush'd and
    chaste;
Where Porphyro took covert, pleas'd amain.
His poor guide hurried back with agues in her
    brain.   62

XXII.

Her falt'ring hand upon the balustrade,
Old Angela was feeling for the stair,
When Madeline, Saint Agnes' charmed maid,
Rose, like a mission'd spirit, unaware;
With silver taper's light, and pious care,
She turn'd, and down the aged gossip led
To a safe level matting. Now prepare,
Young Porphyro, for gazing on that bed;
She comes, she comes again, like ring-dove fray'd
    and fled.

XXIII.

Out went the taper as she hurried in;
Its little smoke, in pallid moonshine, died.
She clos'd the door, she panted, all akin
To spirits of the air, and visions wide:
No utter'd syllable, or, woe betide!
But to her heart, her heart was voluble,
Paining with eloquence her balmy side,—
As though a tongueless nightingale should
    swell
Her throat in vain, and die, heart-stifled, in her
    dell.

XXIV.

A casement high and triple-arch'd there was,
All garlanded with carven imag'ries
Of fruits, and flowers, and bunches of knot-
　　grass,
And diamonded with panes of quaint device,
Innumerable of stains and splendid dyes
As are the tiger-moth's deep-damask'd wings;
And in the midst, 'mong thousand heraldries
And twilight saints, and dim emblazonings,
A　shielded　scutcheon 'blush'd with blood of
　　queens and kings.

XXV.

Full on this casement shone the wintry moon,
And threw warm gules on Madeline's fair breast,
As down she knelt for Heaven's grace and boon;
Rose-bloom fell on her hands, together prest,
And on her silver cross soft amethyst,
And on her hair a glory, like a saint:
She seem'd a splendid angel, newly drest,
Save wings for heaven.　Porphyro grew faint,
She knelt, so pure a thing, so free from mortal
　　taint.

The Eve of Saint Agnes.

XXVI.

Anon his heart revives: her vespers done,
Of all its wreathed pearls her hair she frees;
Unclasps her warmed jewels one by one;
Loosens her fragrant boddice; by degrees
Her rich attire creeps rustling to her knees.
Half-hidden, like a mermaid in sea-weed,
Pensive awhile she dreams awake, and sees,
In fancy, fair Saint Agnes in her bed,
But dares not look behind, or all the charm is
      fled.

XXVII.

Soon, trembling in her soft and chilly nest,
In sort of wakeful swoon, perplex'd she lay,
Until the poppied warmth of sleep oppress'd
Her soothed limbs, and soul fatigued away,—
Flown, like a thought, until the morrow-day;
Blissfully haven'd both from joy and pain;
Clasp'd like a missal where swart Paynims
      pray;
Blinded alike from sunshine and from rain,
As though a rose should shut, and be a bud
      again.

XXVIII.

Stol'n to this paradise, and so entranced,
Porphyro gaz'd upon her empty dress,
And listen'd to her breathing, if it chanced
To wake into a slumberous tenderness;
Which when he heard, that minute did he bless,
And breath'd himself: then from the closet
    crept,
Noiseless as fear in a wide wilderness,
And over the hush'd carpet, silent, stept,
And 'tween the curtains peep'd, where, lo!—
    how fast she slept.

XXIX.

Then by the bed-side, where the faded moon
Made a dim, silver twilight, soft he set
A table, and, half anguish'd, threw thereon
A cloth of woven crimson, gold and jet.
O for some drowsy Morphean amulet!
The boisterous, midnight, festive clarion,
The kettle-drum, and far-heard clarionet,
Affray his ears, though but in dying tone.
The hall-door shuts again, and all the noise is
    gone.

XXX.

And still she slept an azure-lidded sleep,
In blanched linen, smooth, and lavender'd,
While he from forth the closet brought a
      heap
Of candied apple, quince, and plum, and
      gourd;
With jellies soother than the creamy curd,
And lucent syrups, tinct with cinnamon;
Manna and dates, in argosy transferr'd
From Fez; and spiced dainties, every one,
From silken Samarcand to cedar'd Lebanon.

XXXI.

These delicates he heap'd with glowing hand
On golden dishes and in baskets bright
Of wreathed silver; sumptuous they stand
In the retired quiet of the night,
Filling the chilly room with perfume light.
"And now, my love, my seraph fair, awake!
Thou art my heaven, and I thine eremite!
Open thine eyes, for meek Saint Agnes' sake,
Or I shall drowse beside thee, so my soul doth
      ache."

XXXII.

Thus whispering, his warm, unnerved arm
Sank in her pillow.   Shaded was her dream
By the dusk curtains, — 't was a midnight
    charm
Impossible to melt as iced stream.
The lustrous salvers in the moonlight gleam;
Broad golden fringe upon the carpet lies:
It seem'd he never, never could redeem
From such a steadfast. spell his lady's eyes,
So mused awhile, entoil'd in woofed fantasies.

XXXIII.

Awakening up, he took her hollow lute, —
Tumultuous, — and in chords that tenderest
    be,
He play'd an ancient ditty, long since mute,
In Provence call'd " La belle dame sans mercy : "
Close to her ear touching the melody;
Wherewith disturb'd, she utter'd a soft moan.
He ceas'd, she panted quick, and suddenly
Her blue affrayed eyes wide open shone;
Upon his knees he sank, pale as smooth-sculp-
    tured stone.

"AWAKENING UP, HE TOOK HER HOLLOW LUTE."

The Eve of Saint Agnes.

XXXIV.

Her eyes were open, but she still beheld,
Now wide awake, the vision of her sleep.
There was a painful change that nigh expell'd
The blisses of her dream so pure and deep,
At which fair Madeline began to weep,
And moan forth witless words with many a sigh;
While still her gaze on Porphyro would keep,
Who knelt, with joined hands and piteous eye,
Fearing to move or speak, she look'd so dream-
        ingly.

XXXV.

"Ah, Porphyro!" said she, "but even now
Thy voice was at sweet tremble in mine ear,
Made tuneable with every sweetest vow;
And those sad eyes were spiritual and clear.
How changed thou art! how pallid, chill, and
        drear!
Give me that voice again, my Porphyro,
Those looks immortal, those complainings dear!
Oh leave me not in this eternal woe,
For if thou diest, my Love, I know not where
        to go!"

XXXVI.

Beyond a mortal man impassion'd far
At these voluptuous accents, he arose,
Ethereal, flush'd, and like a throbbing star
Seen 'mid the sapphire heaven's deep repose;
Into her dream he melted, as the rose
Blendeth its odor with the violet, —
Solution sweet. Meantime the frost-wind blows
Like Love's alarum, pattering the sharp sleet
Against the window-panes; Saint Agnes' moon
      hath set.

XXXVII.

'T is dark; quick pattereth the flaw-blown
      sleet.
"This is no dream, my bride, my Madeline!"
'Tis dark; the iced gusts still rave and beat.
"No dream, alas! alas! and woe is mine!
Porphyro will leave me here to fade and pine.
Cruel, what traitor could thee hither bring?
I curse not, for my heart is lost in thine,
Though thou forsakest a deceived thing, —
A dove forlorn and lost with sick unpruned
      wing."

71

XXXVIII.

" My Madeline, sweet dreamer, lovely bride !
Say, may I be for aye thy vassal blest ;
Thy beauty's shield, heart-shap'd and vermeil
    dy'd ?
Ah, silver shrine, here will I take my rest
After so many hours of toil and quest,
A famish'd pilgrim saved by miracle.
Though I have found, I will not rob thy
    nest
Saving of thy sweet self ; if thou think'st well
To trust, fair Madeline, to no rude infidel.

XXXIX.

"Hark ! 'tis an elfin storm from faery land,
Of haggard seeming, but a boon indeed.
Arise — arise ! the morning is at hand ;
The bloated wassailers will never heed :
Let us away, my love, with happy speed ;
There are no ears to hear, or eyes to see, —
Drown'd all in Rhenish and the sleepy mead.
Awake ! arise ! my love, and fearless be,
For o'er the southern moors I have a home for
    thee."

72

XL.

She hurried at his words, beset with fears,
For there were sleeping dragons all around,
At glaring watch, perhaps, with ready spears.
Down the wide stairs a darkling way they
    found.
In all the house was heard no human sound.
A chain-droop'd lamp was flickering by each
    door;
The arras, rich with horseman, hawk, and hound,
Flutter'd in the besieging wind's uproar;
And the long carpets rose along the gusty floor.

XLI.

They glide, like phantoms, into the wide hall;
Like phantoms to the iron porch they glide,
Where lay the Porter, in uneasy sprawl,
With a huge empty flagon by his side.
The wakeful bloodhound rose, and shook his
    hide,
But his sagacious eye an inmate owns.
By one and one, the bolts full easy slide;
The chains lie silent on the footworn stones;
The key turns, and the door upon its hinges
    groans.   73

XLII.

And they are gone: ay, ages long ago
These lovers fled away into the storm.
That night the Baron dreamt of many a woe,
And all his warrior-guests, with shade and form
Of witch and demon and large coffin-worm,
Were long be-nightmar'd. Angela the old
Died palsy-twitch'd, with meagre face deform;
The Beadsman, after thousand aves told,
For aye unsought for slept among his ashes cold.

LAMIA

LAMIA

PART I.

UPON a time, before the faery broods
    Drove Nymph and Satyr from the pros-
       perous woods,
Before King Oberon's bright diadem,
Sceptre, and mantle, clasp'd with dewy gem,
Frighted away the Dryads and the Fauns
From rushes green and brakes and cowslip'd
       lawns,

Lamia.

The ever-smitten Hermes empty left
His golden throne, bent warm on amorous theft:
From high Olympus had he stolen light,
On this side of Jove's clouds, to escape the sight
Of his great summoner, and made retreat
Into a forest on the shores of Crete.
For somewhere in that sacred island dwelt
A nymph to whom all hoofed Satyrs knelt,
At whose white feet the languid Tritons poured
Pearls, while on land they wither'd and adored.
Fast by the springs where she to bathe was wont,
And in those meads where sometimes she might
                haunt,
Were strewn rich gifts, unknown to any Muse,
Though Fancy's casket were unlock'd to choose.
Ah, what a world of love was at her feet!
So Hermes thought, and a celestial heat
Burnt from his winged heels to either ear,
That from a whiteness as the lily clear
Blush'd into roses 'mid his golden hair,
Fallen in jealous curls about his shoulders bare.

From vale to vale, from wood to wood, he flew,
Breathing upon the flowers his passion new,

And wound with many a river to its head,
To find where this sweet nymph prepar'd her
    secret bed.
In vain; the sweet nymph might nowhere be
    found;
And so he rested on the lonely ground,
Pensive, and full of painful jealousies
Of the Wood-Gods, and even the very trees.
There as he stood he heard a mournful voice,
Such as, once heard, in gentle heart destroys
All pain but pity. Thus the lone voice spake:
"When from this wreathed tomb shall I awake?
When move in a sweet body fit for life,
And love and pleasure and the ruddy strife
Of hearts and lips? Ah, miserable me!"
The God, dove-footed, glided silently
Round bush and tree, soft-brushing, in his
    speed,
The taller grasses and full-flowering weed,
Until he found a palpitating snake,
Bright and cirque-couchant in a dusky brake.

   She was a Gordian shape of dazzling hue.
Vermilion-spotted, golden, green, and blue;

Lamia.

Strip'd like a zebra, freckled like a pard,
Ey'd like a peacock, and all crimson barr'd;
And full of silver moons, that, as she breathed,
Dissolved or brighter shone or interwreathed
Their lustres with the gloomier tapestries, —
So rainbow-sided, touch'd with miseries,
She seem'd at once, some penanc'd lady elf,
Some demon's mistress, or the demon's self.
Upon her crest she wore a wannish fire
Sprinkled with stars, like Ariadne's tiar;
Her head was serpent, but ah, bitter-sweet!
She had a woman's mouth with all its pearls
        complete;
And for her eyes: what could such eyes do there
But weep, and weep, that they were born so fair?
As Proserpine still weeps for her Sicilian air.
Her throat was serpent, but the words she spake
Came, as through bubbling honey, for Love's sake;
And thus, while Hermes on his pinions lay,
Like a stoop'd falcon ere he takes his prey.

  "Fair Hermes crown'd with feathers, flutter-
        ing light,
I had a splendid dream of thee last night:

I saw thee sitting, on a throne of gold,
Among the Gods, upon Olympus old,
The only sad one; for thou didst not hear
The soft, lute-finger'd Muses chanting clear,
Nor even Apollo when he sang alone,
Deaf to his throbbing throat's long, long melo-
   dious moan.
I dreamt I saw thee, rob'd in purple flakes,
Break amorous through the clouds, as morning
   breaks,
And, swiftly as a bright Phœbean dart,
Strike for the Cretan isle; and here thou art!
Too gentle Hermes, hast thou found the maid?"
Whereat the star of Lethe not delay'd
His rosy eloquence, and thus inquired:
" Thou smooth-lipp'd serpent, surely high-in-
   spired!
Thou beauteous wreath, with melancholy eyes,
Possess whatever bliss thou canst devise,
Telling me only where my nymph is fled, — .
Where she doth breathe!" " Bright planet, thou
   hast said,"
Return'd the snake, " but seal with oaths, fair God!"
" I swear," said Hermes, " by my serpent rod,

And by thine eyes, and by thy starry crown!"
Light flew his earnest words, among the blossoms
    blown.
Then thus again the brilliance feminine:
"Too frail of heart! for this lost nymph of
    thine,
Free as the air, invisably she strays
About these thornless wilds; her pleasant days
She tastes unseen; unseen her nimble feet
Leave traces in the grass and flowers sweet;
From weary tendrils, and bow'd branches green,
She plucks the fruit unseen. she bathes unseen:
And by my power is her beauty veil'd
To keep it unaffronted, unassail'd
By the love-glances of unlovely eyes
Of Satyrs, Fauns, and blear'd Silenus' sighs.
Pale grew her immortality, for woe
Of all these lovers, and she grieved so
I took compassion on her, bade her steep
Her hair in weird syrups, that would keep
Her loveliness invisible, yet free
To wander as she loves, in liberty.
Thou shalt behold her, Hermes, thou alone,
If thou wilt, as thou swearest, grant my boon!"

Then, once again, the charmed God began
An oath, and through the serpent's ears it ran
Warm, tremulous, devout, psalterian.
Ravish'd she lifted her Circean head,
Blush'd a live damask, and swift-lisping said,
"I was a woman, let me have once more
A woman's shape, and charming as before.
I love a youth of Corinth — O the bliss!
Give me my woman's form, and place me
    where he is.
Stoop, Hermes, let me breathe upon thy brow,
And thou shalt see thy sweet nymph even now."
The God on half-shut feathers sank serene,
She breath'd upon his eyes, and swift was seen
Of both the guarded nymph near-smiling on
    the green.
It was no dream; or say a dream it was,
Real are the dreams of Gods, and smoothly pass
Their pleasures in a long immortal dream.
One warm, flush'd moment, hovering, it might
    seem
Dash'd by the wood-nymph's beauty, so he
    burn'd;
Then, lighting on the printless verdure, turn'd

Lamia.

To the swoon'd serpent, and with languid arm,
Delicate, put to proof the lythe Caducean charm.
So done, upon the nymph his eyes he bent
Full of adoring tears and blandishment,
And towards her stept. She, like a moon in wane,
Faded before him, cower'd, nor could restrain
Her fearful sobs, self-folding like a flower
That faints into itself at evening hour:
But the God fostering her chilled hand,
She felt the warmth, her eyelids open'd bland,
And, like new flowers at morning song of bees,
Bloom'd, and gave up her honey to the lees.
Into the green-recessed woods they flew;
Nor grew they pale, as mortal lovers do.

Left to herself, the serpent now began
To change; her elfin blood in madness ran,
Her mouth foam'd, and the grass, therewith
        besprent,
Wither'd at dew so sweet and virulent;
Her eyes in torture fix'd, and anguish drear,
Hot, glaz'd, and wide, with lid-lashes all sear,
Flash'd phosphor and sharp sparks, without one
        cooling tear.

The colors all inflam'd throughout her train,
She writhed about, convulsed with scarlet pain;
A deep volcanian yellow took the place
Of all her milder-mooned body's grace;
And as the lava ravishes the mead,
Spoilt all her silver mail, and golden brede;
Made gloom of all her frecklings, streaks, and bars,
Eclips'd her crescents, and lick'd up her stars:
So that, in moments few, she was undrest
Of all her sapphires, greens, and amethyst,
And rubious-argent, — of all these bereft,
Nothing but pain and ugliness were left.
Still shone her crown; that vanish'd, also she
Melted and disappear'd as suddenly;
And in the air, her new voice luting soft,
Cry'd, " Lycius, gentle Lycius ! " — borne aloft
With the bright mists about the mountains hoar
These words dissolv'd : Crete's forests heard no
    more.

Whither fled Lamia, now a lady bright,
A full-born beauty new and exquisite ?
She fled into that valley they pass o'er
Who go to Corinth from Cenchreas' shore;

Lamia.

And rested at the foot of those wild hills
The rugged founts of the Peræan rills,
And of that other ridge whose barren back
Stretches, with all its mist and cloudy rack,
South-westward to Cleone. There she stood,
About a young bird's flutter from a wood,
Fair, on a sloping green of mossy tread,
By a clear pool, wherein she passioned
To see herself escap'd from so sore ills,
While her robes flaunted with the daffodils.

Ah, happy Lycius!—for she was a maid
More beautiful than ever twisted braid,
Or sigh'd, or blush'd, or on spring-flowered lea
Spread a green kirtle to the minstrelsy;
A virgin purest lipp'd, yet in the lore
Of love deep learned to the red heart's core,—
Not one hour old, yet of sciential brain
To unperplex bliss from its neighbor pain,
Define their pettish limits, and estrange
Their points of contact, and swift counterchange:
Intrigue with the specious chaos, and dispart
Its most ambiguous atoms with sure art;
As though in Cupid's college she had spent

Sweet days a lovely graduate, still unshent,
And kept his rosy terms in idle languishment.

    Why this fair creature chose so faerily
By the wayside to linger, we shall see;
But first 't is fit to tell how she could muse
And dream, when in the serpent prison-house,
Of all she list, strange or magnificent:
How, ever, where she will'd, her spirit went, —
Whether to faint Elysium, or where
Down through tress-lifting waves the Nereids fair
Wind into Thetis' bower by many a pearly stair;
Or where God Bacchus drains his cups divine,
Stretch'd out, at ease, beneath a glutinous pine;
Or where in Pluto's gardens palatine
Mulciber's columns gleam in far piazzian line.
And sometimes into cities she would send
Her dream, with feast and rioting to blend;
And once, while among mortals dreaming thus,
She saw the young Corinthian Lycius
Charioting foremost in the envious race,
Like a young Jove with calm uneager face,
And fell into a swooning love of him.
Now on the moth-time of that evening dim

He would return that way, as well she knew,
To Corinth from the shore; for freshly blew
The eastern soft wind, and his galley now
Grated the quay-stones with her brazen prow
In port Cenchreas, from Egina Isle
Fresh anchor'd; whither he had been awhile
To sacrifice to Jove, whose temple there
Waits with high marble doors for blood and
    incense rare.
Jove heard his vows, and better'd his desire;
For by some freakful chance he made retire
From his companions, and set forth to walk,
Perhaps grown wearied of their Corinth talk;
Over the solitary hills he fared,
Thoughtless, at first, but ere eve's star appear'd
His fantasy was lost, where reason fades,
In the calm'd twilight of Platonic shades.
Lamia beheld him coming, near, more near,
Close to her passing, in indifference drear;
His silent sandals swept the mossy green;
So neighbor'd to him, and yet so unseen,
She stood. He pass'd, shut up in mysteries,
His mind wrapp'd like his mantle, while her
    eyes

Follow'd his steps, and her neck regal white
Turn'd, syllabling thus, "Ah, Lycius bright,
And will you leave me on the hills alone?
Lycius, look back, and be some pity shown!"
He did; not with cold wonder fearingly,
But Orpheus-like at an Eurydice;
For so delicious were the words she sung,
It seem'd he had loved them a whole summer long.
And soon his eyes had drunk her beauty up,
Leaving no drop in the bewildering cup,
And still the cup was full; while he, afraid
Lest she should vanish ere his lip had paid
Due adoration, thus began to adore,
Her soft look growing coy, she saw his chain
      so sure:
" Leave thee alone ! Look back ! Ah, Goddess, see
Whether my eyes can ever turn from thee !
For pity do not this sad heart belie —
Even as thou vanishest so I shall die.
Stay, though a Naiad of the rivers, stay !
To thy far wishes will thy streams obey.
Stay, though the greenest woods be thy domain,
Alone they can drink up the morning rain !
Though a descended Pleiad, will not one

Of thine harmonious sisters keep in tune
Thy spheres, and as thy silver proxy shine?
So sweetly to these ravish'd ears of mine
Came thy sweet greeting, that if thou shouldst
      fade
Thy memory will waste me to a shade, —
For pity do not melt!" "If I should stay,"
Said Lamia, "here, upon this floor of clay,
And pain my steps upon these flowers too rough,
What canst thou say or do of charm enough
To dull the nice remembrance of my home?
Thou canst not ask me with thee here to roam
Over these hills and vales, where no joy is, —
Empty of immortality and bliss!
Thou art a scholar, Lycius, and must know
That finer spirits cannot breathe below
In human climes, and live. Alas, poor youth,
What taste of purer air hast thou to soothe
My essence? What serener palaces,
Where I may all my many senses please
And by mysterious sleights a hundred thirsts
      appease?
It cannot be. Adieu!" So said, she rose
Tiptoe, with white arms spread. He, sick to lose

The amorous promise of her lone complain,
Swoon'd, murmuring of love and pale with pain.
The cruel lady, without any show
Of sorrow for her tender favorite's woe,
But rather, if her eyes could brighter be,
With brighter eyes and slow amenity
Put her new lips to his, and gave afresh
The life she had so tangled in her mesh;
And as he from one trance was wakening
Into another, she began to sing,
Happy in beauty, life, and love, and everything,
A song of love, too sweet for earthly lyres,
While, like held breath, the stars drew in their
          panting fires.
And then she whisper'd in such trembling tone,
As those who, safe together met alone
For the first time through many anguish'd days,
Use other speech than looks; bidding him raise
His drooping head, and clear his soul of doubt,
For that she was a woman, and without
Any more subtle fluid in her veins
Than throbbing blood, and that the self-same pains
Inhabited her frail-strung heart as his.
And next she wonder'd how his eyes could miss

Her face so long in Corinth, where, she said,
She dwelt but half retir'd, and there had led
Days happy as the gold coin could invent
Without the aid of love; yet in content
Till she saw him, as once she pass'd him by,
Where 'gainst a column he leant thoughtfully
At Venus' temple porch, 'mid baskets heap'd
Of amorous herbs and flowers, newly reap'd
Late on that eve, as 't was the night before
The Adonian feast; whereof she saw no more,
But wept alone those days, for why should she
      adore?
Lycius from death awoke into amaze,
To see her still, and singing so sweet lays;
Then from amaze into delight he fell
To hear her whisper woman's lore so well;
And every word she spake entic'd him on
To unperplex'd delight and pleasure known.
Let the mad poets say whate'er they please
Of the sweets of Faeries, Peris, Goddesses,
There is not such a treat among them all,
Haunters of cavern, lake, and waterfall,
As a real woman, lineal indeed
From Pyrrha's pebbles or old Adam's seed.

"AT VENUS' TEMPLE PORCH 'MID BASKETS HEAP'D."

Thus gentle Lamia judg'd, and judg'd aright,
That Lycius could not love in half a fright,
So threw the goddess off, and won his heart
More pleasantly by playing woman's part,
With no more awe than what her beauty
      gave,
That, while it smote, still guaranteed to save.
Lycius to all made eloquent reply,
Marrying to every word a twin-born sigh;
And last, pointing to Corinth, ask'd her sweet,
If 't was too far that night for her soft feet.
The way was short, for Lamia's eagerness
Made, by a spell, the triple league decrease
To a few paces; not at all surmised
By blinded Lycius, so in her comprised.
They pass'd the city gates, he knew not how,
So noiseless, and he never thought to know.

   As men talk in a dream, so Corinth all,
Throughout her palaces imperial,
And all her populous streets and temples lewd,
Mutter'd, like tempest in the distance brew'd,
To the wide-spreaded night above her towers.
Men, women, rich and poor, in the cool hours,

Shuffled their sandals o'er the pavement white,
Companion'd or alone; while many a light
Flar'd, here and there, from wealthy festivals,
And threw their moving shadows on the walls,
Or found them cluster'd in the corniced shade
Of some arch'd temple door, or dusky colonnade.

Muffling his face, of greeting friends in fear,
Her fingers he press'd hard, as one came near
With curl'd gray beard, sharp eyes, and smooth
      bald crown,
Slow-stepp'd, and rob'd in philosophic gown.
Lycius shrank closer, as they met and past,
Into his mantle, adding wings to haste,
While hurried Lamia trembled: "Ah," said he,
"Why do you shudder, love, so ruefully?
Why does your tender palm dissolve in dew?"
"I 'm wearied," said fair Lamia: "tell me who
Is that old man? I cannot bring to mind
His features. Lycius, wherefore did you blind
Yourself from his quick eyes?" Lycius reply'd
"'T is Apollonius sage, my trusty guide
And good instructor; but to-night he seems
The ghost of Folly haunting my sweet dreams."

While yet he spake they had arrived before
A pillar'd porch, with lofty portal door,
Where hung a silver lamp, whose phosphor glow
Reflected in the slabbed steps below,
Mild as a star in winter; for so new,
And so unsullied was the marble's hue,
So through the crystal polish, liquid fine,
Ran the dark veins, that none but feet divine
Could e'er have touch'd there. Sounds Æolian
Breath'd from the hinges, as the ample span
Of the wide doors disclos'd a place unknown
Some time to any, but those two alone,
And a few Persian mutes, who that same year
Were seen about the markets: none knew where
They could inhabit; the most curious
Were foil'd, who watch'd to trace them to their
      house:
And but the flitter-winged verse must tell,
For truth's sake, what woe afterwards befell;
'T would humor many a heart to leave them thus,
Shut from the busy world of more incredulous.

PART II.

L OVE in a hut, with water and a crust,
Is — Love, forgive us ! — cinders, ashes, dust;
Love in a palace is perhaps at last
More grievous torment than a hermit's fast, —
That is a doubtful tale from faery land,
Hard for the non-elect to understand.
Had Lycius liv'd to hand his story down,
He might have given the moral a fresh frown,
Or clench'd it quite; but too short was their bliss
To breed distrust and hate, that make the soft
        voice hiss.
Besides, there, nightly, with terrific glare,
Love, jealous grown of so complete a pair,
Hover'd and buzz'd his wings, with fearful roar,
Above the lintel of their chamber door,
And down the passage cast a glow upon the floor.

For all this came a ruin. Side by side
They were enthroned, in the even tide,
Upon a couch near to a curtaining

Whose airy texture, from a golden string,
Floated into the room, and let appear
Unveil'd the summer heaven, blue and clear,
Betwixt two marble shafts, — there they reposed,
Where use had made it sweet, with eyelids
    closed,
Saving a tithe which love still open kept,
That they might see each other while they almost
    slept;
When from the slope side of a suburb hill,
Deafening the swallow's twitter, came a thrill
Of trumpets. Lycius started; the sounds fled,
But left a thought, a buzzing in his head.
For the first time, since first he harbor'd in
That purple-lined palace of sweet sin,
His spirit pass'd beyond its golden bourn
Into the noisy world almost forsworn.
The lady, ever watchful, penetrant,
Saw this with pain, so arguing a want
Of something more, more than her empery
Of joys; and she began to moan and sigh
Because he mus'd beyond her, knowing well
That but a moment's thought is passion's pass-
    ing bell.

"CAME A THRILL
OF TRUMPETS. LYCIUS STARTED; THE SOUNDS FLED."

"Why do you sigh, fair creature?" whisper'd he,
"Why do you think?" return'd she tenderly;
"You have deserted me. Where am i now?
Not in your heart while care weighs on your brow.
No, no, you have dismiss'd me, and I go
From your breast houseless : ay, it must be so."
He answer'd, bending to her open eyes,
Where he was mirror'd small in paradise,
"My silver planet, both of eve and morn,
Why will you plead yourself so sad forlorn,
While I am striving how to fill my heart
With deeper crimson and a double smart?
How to entangle, trammel up, and snare
Your soul in mine, and labyrinth you there
Like the hid scent in an unbudded rose?
Ay, a sweet kiss — you see your mighty woes.
My thoughts, shall I unveil them? Listen then!
What mortal hath a prize, that other men
May be confounded and abash'd withal,
But lets it sometimes pace abroad majestical,
And triumph, as in thee I should rejoice
Amid the hoarse alarm of Corinth's voice.
Let my foes choke, and my friends shout afar,
While through the thronged streets your bridal car

Wheels round its dazzling spokes." The lady's
    cheek
Trembled; she nothing said, but pale and meek,
Arose and knelt before him, wept a rain
Of sorrows at his words; at last with pain
Beseeching him, the while his hand she wrung,
To change his purpose. He thereat was stung,
Perverse, with stronger fancy to reclaim
Her wild and timid nature to his aim.
Besides, for all his love, in self despite,
Against his better self, he took delight
Luxurious in her sorrows, soft and new.
His passion, cruel grown, took on a hue
Fierce and sanguineous as 't was possible
In one whose brow had no dark veins to swell.
Fine was the mitigated fury, like
Apollo's presence when in act to strike
The serpent — Ha, the serpent! certes, she
Was none. She burnt, she loved the tyranny,
And, all subdued, consented to the hour
When to the bridal he should lead his paramour.
Whispering in midnight silence, said the youth,
"Sure some sweet name thou hast, though, by
    my truth,

I have not ask'd it, ever thinking thee
Not mortal, but of heavenly progeny,
As still I do.   Hast any mortal name,
Fit appellation for this dazzling frame?
Or friends or kinsfolk on the citied earth,
To share our marriage feast and nuptial mirth?"
"I have no friends," said Lamia, "no, not one;
My presence in wide Corinth hardly known.
My parents' bones are in their dusty urns
Sepulchred, where no kindled incense burns,
Seeing all their luckless race are dead, save me,
And I neglect the holy rite for thee.
Even as you list invite your many guests;
But if, as. now it seems, your vision rests
With any pleasure on me, do not bid
Old Apollonius,—from him keep me hid."
Lycius, perplex'd at words so blind and blank,
Made close inquiry; from whose touch she
        shrank,
Feigning a sleep; and he to the dull shade
Of deep sleep in a moment was betray'd.

It was the custom then to bring away
The bride from home at blushing shut of day,

Veil'd, in a chariot, heralded along
By strewn flowers, torches, and a marriage song,
With other pageants; but this fair unknown
Had not a friend. So being left alone
(Lycius was gone to summon all his kin)
And knowing surely she could never win
His foolish heart from its mad pompousness,
She set herself, high-thoughted, how to dress
The misery in fit magnificence.
She did so, but 't is doubtful how and whence
Came, and who were her subtle servitors.
About the halls, and to and from the doors,
There was a noise of wings, till in short space
The glowing banquet-room shone with wide-
    arched grace.
A haunting music, sole perhaps and lone
Supportress of the faery-roof, made moan
Throughout, as fearful the whole charm might
    fade.
Fresh carved cedar, mimicking a glade
Of palm and plantain, met from either side,
High in the midst, in honor of the bride:
Two palms and then two plantains, and so on,
From either side their stems branch'd one to one

All down the aisled place; and beneath all
There ran a stream of lamps straight on from
     wall to wall.
So canopy'd, lay an untasted feast
Teeming with odors. Lamia, regal drest,
Silently pac'd about, and as she went,
In pale contented sort of discontent,
Mission'd her viewless servants to enrich
The fretted splendor of each nook and niche.
Between the tree-stems, marbled plain at first,
Came jasper panels; then anon there burst
Forth creeping imagery of slighter trees,
And with the larger wove in small intricacies,
Approving all, she faded at self-will,
And shut the chamber up, close, hush'd, and
     still,
Complete and ready for the revels rude,
When dreadful guests would come to spoil her
     solitude.

The day appear'd, and all the gossip rout,
O senseless Lycius! Madman, wherefore flout
The silent-blessing fate, warm cloister'd hours,
And show to common eyes'these secret bowers?

The herd approach'd; each guest, with busy brain,
Arriving at the portal, gaz'd amain,
And enter'd marvelling; for they knew the street,
Remember'd it from childhood all complete
Without a gap, yet ne'er before had seen
That royal porch, that high-built fair demesne;
So in they hurried all, maz'd, curious and
    keen:
Save one, who look'd thereon with eye severe,
And with calm-planted steps walk'd in austere,—
'T was Apollonius. Something too he laugh'd,
As though some knotty problem, that had daft
His patient thought, had now begun to thaw,
And solve and melt: 'T was just as he foresaw.

He met within the murmurous vestibule
His young disciple. "'T is no common rule,
Lycius," said he, "for uninvited guest
To force himself upon you, and infest
With an unbidden presence the bright throng
Of younger friends; yet must I do this wrong,
And you forgive me." Lycius blush'd, and led
The old man through the inner doors broad-
    spread;

With reconciling words and courteous mien
Turning into sweet milk the sophist's spleen.

Of wealthy lustre was the banquet-room,
Fill'd with pervading brilliance and perfume:
Before each lucid panel fuming stood
A censer fed with myrrh and spiced wood,
Each by a sacred tripod held aloft
Whose slender feet wide-swerv'd upon the soft
Wool-woofed carpets; fifty wreaths of smoke
From fifty censers their light voyage took
To the high roof, still mimick'd as they rose
Along the mirror'd walls by twin-clouds odorous.
Twelve sphered tables, by silk seats inspher'd,
High as the level of a man's breast rear'd
On libbard's paws, upheld the heavy gold
Of cups and goblets, and the store thrice told
Of Ceres' horn, and, in huge vessels, wine
Come from the gloomy tun with merry shine.
Thus loaded with a feast the tables stood,
Each shrining in the midst the image of a God.

When in an antechamber every guest
Had felt the cold full sponge to pleasure press'd,

By minist'ring slaves, upon his hands and feet,
And fragrant oils with ceremony meet
Pour'd on his hair, they all mov'd to the feast
In white robes, and themselves in order plac'd
Around the silken couches, wondering
Whence all this mighty cost and blaze of wealth
    could spring.

Soft went the music the soft air along,
While fluent Greek a vowel'd undersong
Kept up among the guests, discoursing low
At first, for scarcely was the wine at flow;
But when the happy vintage touch'd their brains,
Louder they talk, and louder come the strains
Of powerful instruments. The gorgeous dyes,
The space, the splendor of the draperies,
The roof of awful richness, nectarous cheer,
Beautiful slaves, and Lamia's self appear,
Now, when the wine has done its rosy deed,
And every soul from human trammels freed,
No more so strange; for merry wine, sweet wine,
Will make Elysian shades not too fair, too divine.
Soon was God Bacchus at meridian height;
Flush'd were their cheeks, and bright eyes double
    bright.   107

Lamia.

Garlands of every green and every scent
From vales deflower'd or forest-trees branch-rent,
In baskets of bright osier'd gold were brought
High as the handles heap'd, to suit the thought
Of every guest; that each, as he did please,
Might fancy-fit his brows, silk-pillow'd at his
    ease.

    What wreath for Lamia? What for Lycius?
What for the sage, old Apollonius?
Upon her aching forehead be there hung
The leaves of willow and of adder's tongue;
And for the youth, quick, let us strip for him
The thyrsus, that his watching eyes may swim
Into forgetfulness; and for the sage,
Let spear-grass and the spiteful thistle wage
War on his temples. Do not all charms fly
At the mere touch of cold philosophy?
There was an awful rainbow once in heaven:
We know her woof, her texture; she is given
In the dull catalogue of common things,
Philosophy will clip an Angel's wings,
Conquer all mysteries by rule and line,
Empty the haunted air and gnomed mine,

"TILL, CHECKING HIS LOVE-TRANCE, HE TOOK A CUP,
FULL BRIMM'D."

Unweave a rainbow, as it erewhile made
The tender-person'd Lamia melt into a shade.

By her glad Lycius sitting, in chief place,
Scarce saw in all the room another face,
Till, checking his love trance, a cup he took
Full brimm'd, and opposite sent forth a look
'Cross the broad table, to beseech a glance
From his old teacher's wrinkled countenance,
And pledge him. The bald-head philosopher
Had fix'd his eye, without a twinkle or stir
Full on the alarmed beauty of the bride,
Brow-beating her fair form, and troubling her
        sweet pride.
Lycius then press'd her hand, with devout touch
As pale it lay upon the rosy couch.
'T was icy, and the cold ran through his veins;
Then sudden it grew hot, and all the pains
Of an unnatural heat shot to his heart.
"Lamia, what means this? Wherefore dost thou
        start?
Know'st thou that man?" Poor Lamia answer'd
        not.
He gaz'd into her eyes, and not a jot

Own'd they the lovelorn piteous appeal.
More, more he gazed: his human senses reel;
Some hungry spell that loveliness absorbs;
There was no recognition in those orbs.
"Lamia!" he cried, and no soft-ton'd reply,
The many heard, and the loud revelry
Grew hush; the stately music no more breathes;
The myrtle sicken'd in a thousand wreaths.
By faint degrees voice, lute, and pleasure ceased;
A deadly silence step by step increased,
Until it seem'd a horrid presence there,
And not a man but felt the terror in his hair.
"Lamia!" he shriek'd; and nothing but the shriek
With its sad echo did the silence break.
"Begone, foul dream!" he cry'd, gazing again
In the bride's face, where now no azure vein
Wander'd on fair-spac'd temples; no soft bloom
Misted the cheek; no passion to illume
The deep-recessed vision: — all was blight;
Lamia, no longer fair, there sat a deadly white.
"Shut, shut those juggling eyes, thou ruthless man!
Turn them aside, wretch, or the righteous ban
Of all the Gods, whose dreadful images
Here represent their shadowy presences,

May pierce them on the sudden with the thorn
Of painful blindness, leaving thee forlorn,
In trembling dotage to the feeblest fright
Of conscience, for their long-offended might,
For all thine impious proud-heart sophistries,
Unlawful magic, and enticing lies.
Corinthians, look upon that gray-beard wretch!
Mark how, possess'd, his lashless eyelids stretch
Around his demon eyes! Corinthians, see!
My sweet bride withers at their potency."
"Fool!" said the sophist, in an under-tone
Gruff with contempt; which a death-nighing
        moan
From Lycius answer'd, as heart-struck and lost,
He sank supine beside the aching ghost.
"Fool! Fool!" repeated he, while his eyes still
Relented not, nor mov'd; "from every ill
Of life have I preserv'd thee to this day,
And shall I see thee made a serpent's prey?"
Then Lamia breath'd death breath; the sophist's
        eye,
Like a sharp spear, went through her utterly.
Keen, cruel, perceant, stinging; she, as well
As her weak hand could any meaning tell,

Lamía.

Motion'd him to be silent; vainly so,
He look'd and look'd again a level— No!
" A serpent !" echoed he; no sooner said,
Than with a frightful scream she vanished;
And Lycius' arms were empty of delight,
As were his limbs of life, from that same night.
On the high couch he lay; his friends came
      round,
Supported him: no pulse, or breath they found,
And, in its marriage robe, the heavy body wound.

113

THE END.